Amazing Snakes

Amazing Snakes OF THE Midwest

Parker Holmes

PowerKids press
New York

Published in 2015 by The Rosen Publishing Group, Inc.
29 East 21st Street, New York, NY 10010

Copyright © 2015 by The Rosen Publishing Group, Inc.

All rights reserved. No part of this book may be reproduced in any form without permission in writing from the publisher, except by a reviewer.

First Edition

Editor: Jennifer Way
Book Design: Andrew Povolny
Photo Research: Katie Stryker

Photo Credits: Cover Linda Freshwaters Arndt/Photo Researchers/Getty Images; pp. 5, 21 (bottom) Suzanne L Collins/Photo Researchers/Getty Images; p. 6 John Mitchell/Oxford Scientific/Getty Images; pp. 7, 10 Matt Meadows/Photolibrary/Getty Images; pp. 9, 22 (middle) Suzanne L and Joseph T. Collins/Getty Images; p. 12 Derrick Hamrick/Getty Images; p. 13 Phil Schermeister/National Geographic/Getty Images; pp. 15, 18 James Gerholdt/Photolibrary/Getty Images; p. 16 Larry Miller/Photo Researchers/Getty Images; p. 19 Kenneth M Highfill/Photo Researchers/Getty Images; p. 20 Gerold & Cynthia Merker/Visuals Unlimited, Inc./Visuals Unlimited/Getty Images; p. 21 (top) Wayne Lynch/All Canada Photos/Getty Images; p. 22 (top) James Gerholdt/Stockbyte/Getty Images; p. 22 (bottom) Rex Lisman/Flickr/Getty Images.

Library of Congress Cataloging-in-Publication Data

Holmes, Parker, author.
  Amazing snakes of the Midwest / by Parker Holmes.
      pages cm. — (Amazing snakes)
  Includes index.
  ISBN 978-1-4777-6494-7 (library binding) — ISBN 978-1-4777-6492-3 (pbk.) — ISBN 978-1-4777-6497-8 (6-pack)
  1. Snakes—Middle West—Juvenile literature. I. Title.
  QL666.O6H75 2015
  597.96'0977—dc23
                            2013044856

Manufactured in the United States of America

CPSIA Compliance Information: Batch #WS14PK6: For Further Information contact Rosen Publishing, New York, New York at 1-800 237-9932

Contents

Snakes of the Heartland	4
Fox Snake	6
Eastern Massasauga	8
Blue Racer	10
Bull Snake	12
Plains Garter Snake	14
Ringneck Snake	16
Hognose	18
What's Your Favorite Kind?	20
Other Snakes in the Midwest	22
Glossary	23
Index	24
Websites	24

Snakes of the Heartland

Have you ever seen a snake? If you live in the Midwest, you can see a variety of them. You could see something as big as a 6-foot (2 m) bull snake or as tiny as a 6-inch (15 cm) worm snake. This **region** has close to 40 **species** of snakes. Most of them are harmless, but you may occasionally spot a **venomous** one. Venomous snakes are what many people call poisonous snakes.

If you do see a venomous snake here, there's a good chance it's a rattlesnake. Watch out! Eastern massasaugas and timber rattlesnakes are two kinds you might find. In the most western states of the region, you might come across a prairie rattlesnake. Throughout the Midwest, though, you're more likely to see a harmless species, such as a brown, ribbon, green, garter, or water snake. Let's take a look at some exciting snakes that live around the Midwest!

Ringneck snakes are found throughout North America. They live in woodlands in the Midwest.

Fox Snake

If you run across a fox snake, at first you might think it's a rattlesnake. These nonvenomous **reptiles** don't have rattles, but they vibrate their tails against the ground if they feel **threatened**. They also **coil** up like rattlesnakes. If all this shaking and coiling doesn't scare away the threat, they might spray a stinky **musk**. Yuck! They're called fox snakes because some people think their scent smells like the musk of a fox.

Here, a fox snake is constricting a rat. It will eat the rat whole once it is dead.

The eastern fox snake, shown here, is listed as a threatened species due to habitat loss. That means its numbers are declining because there are fewer places that it can make its home.

Fox snakes are part of the rat snake group. People sometimes call them pine snakes, spotted adders, or timber snakes. There are two kinds of fox snakes: western and eastern. The western fox snake is more common. Fox snakes usually grow to 3 or 4 feet (.9–1.2 m) or larger. They're typically yellow or brown with darker blotches. Fox snakes are constrictors, which means they squeeze their prey to death.

Eastern Massasauga

The eastern massasauga is one of the few venomous snakes in the Midwest. It's a type of rattlesnake, which means it has rattles on the end of its tail. It shakes these rattles to scare off threats. Massasaugas like to live near swamps. That's how they got their name. The name "massasauga" comes from a Native American Chippewa word used to describe swampy areas near rivers. The word is pronounced ma-suh-SAW-guh. These snakes have been nicknamed swamp rattlers and black rattlers. Sometimes they're dark colored, but other times they're light brown or gray with blotches.

Massasaugas are **endangered** in many parts of the Midwest. They're usually about 2 feet (61 cm) long, which is smaller than many other rattlesnakes. They're also shy and not as aggressive as some other rattlesnakes. They're still venomous, though, so don't get too close!

The eastern massasauga's range stretches from the upper Midwest into parts of Canada.

Blue Racer

10

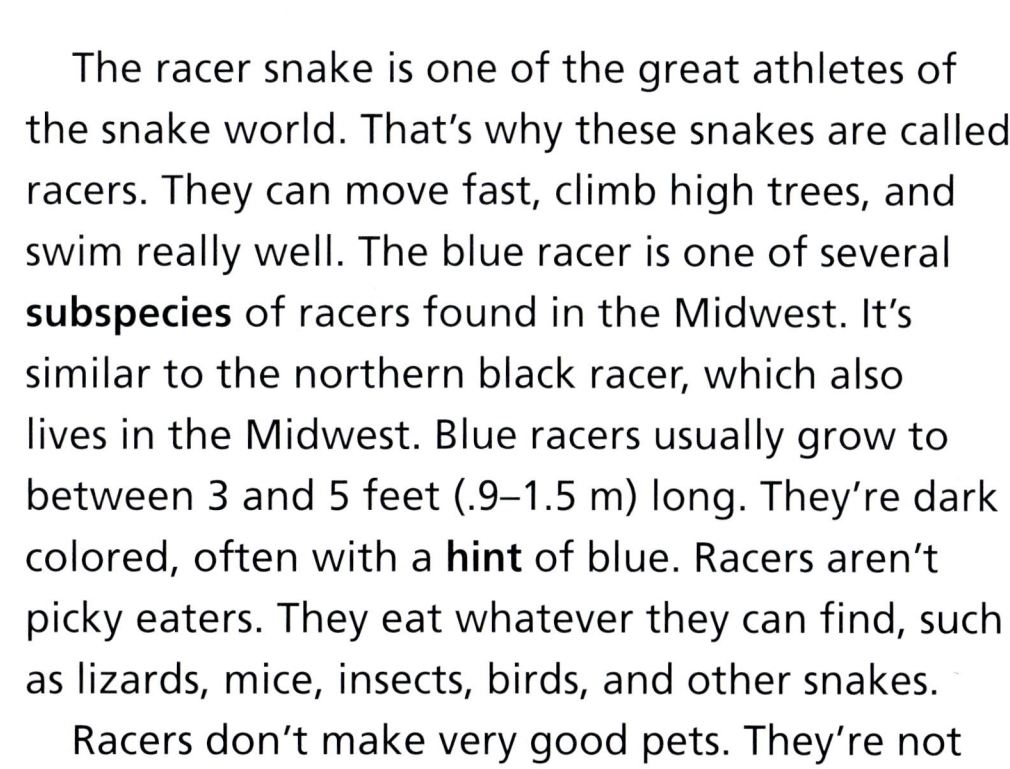

The racer snake is one of the great athletes of the snake world. That's why these snakes are called racers. They can move fast, climb high trees, and swim really well. The blue racer is one of several **subspecies** of racers found in the Midwest. It's similar to the northern black racer, which also lives in the Midwest. Blue racers usually grow to between 3 and 5 feet (.9–1.5 m) long. They're dark colored, often with a **hint** of blue. Racers aren't picky eaters. They eat whatever they can find, such as lizards, mice, insects, birds, and other snakes.

Racers don't make very good pets. They're not venomous, but they're **feisty** snakes that often bite if you pick them up. As a warning to stay away, racers will vibrate their tails on the ground. This creates a buzz that sounds kind of like a rattlesnake's rattle.

Most racers live in grassy or lightly wooded areas.

Bull Snake

A lot of snakes hiss—ssssss! But did you know that bull snakes are one of the best hissers around? They hiss really loudly, and they do it if they feel threatened. These hissing snakes are some of the biggest snakes found in the Midwest. They often grow to around 5 feet (1.5 m), but they can be bigger. The biggest bull snake ever found was huge at 8.5 feet (2.6 m) long!

This bull snake is eating a rabbit.

Here is a bull snake in a grassy area in North Dakota.

Bull snakes are a type of gopher snake, so people sometimes just call them gopher snakes. They can burrow into the ground or hang out in gopher holes. Guess what they enjoy for dinner? These constrictors like to eat **rodents**, such as gophers, mice, and rats. Bull snakes are often brown or yellowish with dark blotches. People sometimes confuse them with rattlesnakes. If you see a big bull snake hissing at you, it may look scary, but don't worry. It's not venomous.

Plains Garter Snake

If you find a snake in the Midwest, it just might be a garter snake. Garter snakes are one of the most common species here. They're also one of the most common snakes throughout the country. The plains garter is one of several types of garter snakes in the Midwest. It looks similar to another common midwestern snake—the eastern garter. Some people call these snakes garden snakes, but they're actually called garters. Plains garter snakes usually grow to around 2 feet (61 cm). They have dark bodies with yellow or orange stripes. These snakes are often found in open areas, such as prairies and meadows. They love to eat insects and frogs.

Plains garter snakes are harmless to people, but they sometimes bite when picked up. These snakes also have another way of defending themselves. They might squirt you with stinky musk and poop. Yikes!

The western plains garter snake, shown here, lives throughout the Midwest, including in Minnesota, Wisconsin, Indiana, and South Dakota.

Ringneck Snake

This prairie ringneck snake is coiled up. This is a pose it takes when it prepares to defend itself.

Ringneck snakes are **expert** hiders. They're common snakes in the Midwest, but unless you're looking for them, you might not see one. They're secretive little snakes that like to hide during the day, often under rocks or inside rotting logs. They usually come out only at night. Can you guess why they're called ringneck snakes? They have colored rings around their necks. Their bodies are dark, but their neck rings and bellies are yellow, orange, or red. There are several varieties of ringneck snakes. The most common kinds in the Midwest are prairie and northern ringnecks. They're usually 10 to 14 inches (25–36 cm) long.

Ringneck snakes eat tiny frogs, salamanders, and other small critters. If they feel threatened, ringnecks will sometimes twist their tails and raise them in the air. These harmless snakes rarely bite people, but if you pick one up, it might release a stinky smell. Be careful!

Hognose

Hognose snakes may be the best actors of the snake world. If they feel threatened, they'll put on quite a show to make you go away. These harmless snakes are only about 2 feet (61 cm) long, but they'll try to scare away a threat by acting big and bad. They'll spread their necks sort of like a cobra does, open their mouths, and hiss. If that doesn't work, they roll on their backs, flop out their tongues, and act dead. Bravo!

The eastern hognose snake has lots of nicknames, including the spreading adder and the deaf adder.

When it feels threatened, the hognose snake can roll over, stick out its tongue, and play dead. This is one of its defense strategies.

There are two species of hognose snakes in the Midwest: the eastern and the plains hognose. Hognose snakes can be dark colored or checkered with various colors. These snakes love to eat toads. That's their favorite meal. Do you know why they're called hognose snakes? Their noses are kind of upturned and broad, like the **snouts** of hogs.

What's Your Favorite Kind?

You can find all kinds of interesting snakes in the Midwest. If you're anywhere near water, you might spot a northern water snake or queen snake. Or you might see a red milk snake hanging out near a farm, looking for a mouse to eat. If you're walking through the woods in the southern part of the region, you might come across a venomous copperhead. Don't get too close!

The red milk snake is a nonvenomous snake that lives throughout the Midwest.

The prairie rattlesnake is found in the Midwest's plains.

But remember—most snakes in the Midwest are harmless. In fact, snakes are good to have around because they eat lots of rodents and insects.

You won't see snakes here all the time. The Midwest can get cold, and snakes don't like chilly weather. They **hibernate** during the winter. But when the weather warms up, you might get to see one. What type would you like to find? The Midwest has lots of exciting snakes!

The queen snake lives in the Midwest as well as the Northeast and Southeast, in the United States.

Other Snakes in the Midwest

- Black rat snake
- Brown snake
- Butler's garter snake
- Common ribbon snake
- Diamondback water snake
- Eastern black king snake
- Eastern milk snake
- Flat-headed snake
- Graham's crayfish snake
- Great Plains rat snake
- Kansas glossy snake
- Kirtland's snake
- Lined snake
- Northern water snake
- Plain-bellied water snake
- Plains black-headed snake
- Red-bellied snake
- Rough green snake
- Smooth earth snake
- Smooth green snake
- Timber rattlesnake
- Worm snake

Eastern milk snake

Kirtland's snake

Rough green snake

Glossary

coil (KOYL) To curl up.

endangered (in-DAYN-jerd) Describing an animal whose species or group has almost all died out.

expert (EK-spert) One who is very good at something.

feisty (FY-stee) Quick to fight or show aggression.

hibernate (HY-bur-nayt) To spend the winter in a sleeplike state.

hint (HINT) A very little bit.

musk (MUSK) Strong-smelling matter given off by an animal's body.

region (REE-jun) Different parts of Earth.

reptiles (REP-tylz) Cold-blooded animals with lungs and scales.

rodents (ROH-dents) Animals with gnawing teeth, such as mice.

snouts (SNOWTS) Animals' noses.

species (SPEE-sheez) A single kind of living thing. All people are one species.

subspecies (SUB-spee-sheez) Types within a species.

threatened (THREH-tund) Acted as though something will possibly cause hurt.

venomous (VEH-nuh-mis) Having a poisonous bite.

Index

B
blotches, 7–8, 13

C
constrictors, 7, 13

E
eastern massasauga(s), 4, 8

K
kinds, 4, 7, 17, 20

M
musk, 6, 14

R
rattle(s), 6, 8, 11
rattlesnake(s), 4, 6, 8, 13, 22
region, 4, 20
reptiles, 6
rodents, 13, 21

S
scent, 6
shaking, 6
snouts, 19
species, 4, 14, 19
spotted adders, 7

states, 4
subspecies, 11

T
tail(s), 6, 8, 11, 17
threat(s), 6, 8, 18
type(s), 8, 13–14, 21

V
variety, 4, 17

W
winter, 21

Websites

Due to the changing nature of Internet links, PowerKids Press has developed an online list of websites related to the subject of this book. This site is updated regularly. Please use this link to access the list: www.powerkidslinks.com/amaz/midw/